THIS BLOOMSBURY BOOK

BELONGS TO

....

Just for Jack – M.R.
For Becky and Leo – C.P.

ABOUT DRAGONS
There are two sorts of dragons in the world. Dragons
who breathe fire, and fight.
And non-fire-breathing dragons who often bring good luck.
Both sorts make their dens in high wild places.
(From The Book of Dragons*)*

First published in Great Britain in 2006 by Bloomsbury Publishing Plc
36 Soho Square, London, W1D 3QY

This paperback edition first published in 2006

Text copyright © Marion Rose 2006
Illustrations copyright © Colin Paine 2006
The moral right of the author has been asserted

A CIP catalogue record of this book is available from the British Library

ISBN 0 7475 7729 3
9780747577294

All papers used by Bloomsbury Publishing are natural, recyclable products made
from wood grown in well-managed forests. The manufacturing processes conform to
the environmental regulations of the country of origin.

Printed in China by South China Printing Co.
1 3 5 7 9 10 8 6 4 2

Designed by Nina Tara

www.bloomsbury.com

GEORGIE
and the
DRAGON

MARION ROSE
ILLUSTRATED BY COLIN PAINE

BLOOMSBURY
CHILDREN'S
BOOKS

Georgie was running home one day, when a thing fell out of the sky in front of him.
"Ouwch!" the thing howled.

Georgie bent over it.
"Are you alright?" he asked.
"My wing!" the thing gasped.
And Georgie saw that the "thing" was a baby dragon!

"Wa-a-ah!" it wailed. Its wing was scratched.
"Does your mum know where you are?" Georgie asked kindly.
"No-o!" the dragon hiccupped.
"I tried to fly. An' I fell down!!!"
"There, there!" Georgie wrapped
his hanky round the scratch.
"I'm Georgie," he said.

Then he stared up at Far Purple Mountain.
Everyone in Georgie's village KNEW
that a huge, fire-breathing
dragon lived up there.

They had seen its red flames light the night sky.
They had smelt its smoky breath.
And as for its dreadful ROAR . . .
Well, nobody dared go NEAR Far Purple Mountain.

"I'm Galahad," sniffed the dragon,
slipping his claw trustingly into
Georgie's hand. "My mum'll
be roaring mad when she finds
I'm gone. Will you take me home?"

"Home?" asked Georgie nervously.
"There, silly!" said Galahad, pointing
to Far Purple Mountain.
"Er – alright," Georgie gulped.

Georgie and Galahad set off.

It wasn't too long before they came
to the banks of the Raging River.
Its waters swirled and swished.
"A-a-a-argh!" Galahad shrieked.
"I can't cross that."

Secretly, Georgie felt like shrieking too.
(What scared HIM though, was coming face
to face with a fire-breathing dragon!)
But somehow, he had to help
Galahad get across the river.
He looked around.
There was an ordinary yellow flower
growing by itself on the riverbank. Maybe . . .

"Look at that!" he said out loud. "A magic sword flower! They make you brave. No river can harm you if you're carrying one of those!"

"Really? Are you sure this is the right sort?" asked Galahad, giving it a good sniff. "Quite sure," said Georgie firmly.

So Galahad held the sword flower high,
and hand in claw, they stepped into the
whirling water.

Soon they were
scrambling out safely
on to the other bank.
"It works!" cried Galahad,
shaking the water from his scales.
"It really is a magic sword
flower!! My mum'll go
WILD when she sees this!"

Before long Georgie and Galahad
came to the Dark-As-Midnight Forest.
The trees loomed over them.
"OO-oooh!" Galahad shivered with fright.
"I can't go in there!"
Quietly, Georgie shivered too.
(He knew there were dragons near!)
But he had to help Galahad get through the forest.
Aloud he said, "Oh, you can trust the magic sword flower.
The forest won't harm you if you're holding that."
"Really? Are you sure it works for forests too?"
Galahad asked doubtfully.
"Sure as dragons have eggs," said Georgie.

He took Galahad
firmly by the
claw, and they
marched into
the forest.

It was dark. And co-o-old.
And very still. *Rustle!*
"Eek!" squeaked Galahad.

But Galahad held the sword flower
tight, and they climbed on and up
until all at once they came out of the
trees and into the sunlight.

"Hurrah – it worked for the
forest too!" cried Galahad,
dancing up the stony path.
"Not far now, Georgie,"
he called. "We're
nearly home!"
Georgie followed,
watching anxiously for
signs of dragon.

Suddenly Galahad stopped!
Georgie nearly fell over him.
Before them was the Devil's Drop,
a deep deep cleft in the mountain.
"No-o-o-o," Galahad moaned.
"I can't jump that!"

Inside, Georgie moaned too.
(The smell of dragon smoke
was starting to prickle his nose.)
But he couldn't leave Galahad here.
"Trust the sword flower," he said.
"We'll jump after three . . ."
"Georgie – does it really work
for . . . ?" Galahad began.
But Georgie was already counting:

one two three

THUNK!
They landed safely
together on the other side.

"Dear magic sword flower,"
whispered Galahad, hugging it.
"And brave Georgie! Just wait
till we see my mum!"

Just then red flames
lit up the sky.
Smoke filled the air and . . .

ROAR!!!!

Georgie's legs froze in fright.
"Er – G-Galahad," gulped Georgie.
"Is that your mum?"

"Georgie," whispered Galahad, tugging at
his hand, "You're not scared, are you?"
"N-n-no w-way!" stuttered Georgie.
"Because – you can hold the magic
sword flower now, if you like."
"Th-thanks," said Georgie.
So Georgie took the flower.
And together they climbed
the last slope, right up
to the dragon's den . . .

"Why, there you are, my little crumpet!" Galahad's mum cried. "You've brought a friend to tea – and, oh! A flower for me? How GORGEOUS of you to think of that!"

After she had given them tea and toast
(only a little burnt), Galahad's mum dropped
Georgie back in his own village.
How everyone stared!!!

Soon, people far and wide heard
how Georgie climbed Far Purple Mountain.
And came home again – on a dragon's back!!!
Ever since, when the magic sword flowers
bloom, the whole village goes on a Dragon Walk.

Georgie leads the way. Galahad flies out to greet him. His mum welcomes everyone in with open wings, and gives them all toasted marshmallows to eat (only a little singed!).

And Georgie can hardly believe his luck!

Enjoy more fabulous books from Bloomsbury Children's Books . . .

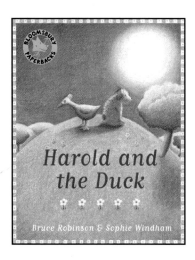

Harold and the Duck

Bruce Robinson and Sophie Windham

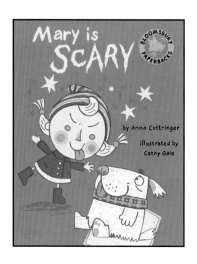

Mary is Scary

Anne Cottringer and Cathy Gale

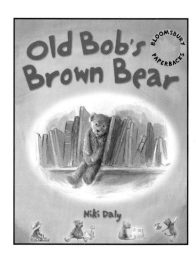

Old Bob's Brown Bear

Niki Daly

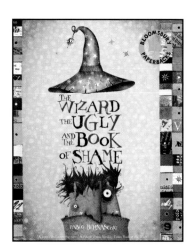

**The Wizard, The Ugly,
and the Book of Shame**

Pablo Bernasconi

The Christmas Tree Fairy

Marion Rose and Jason Cockcroft

All now available in paperback